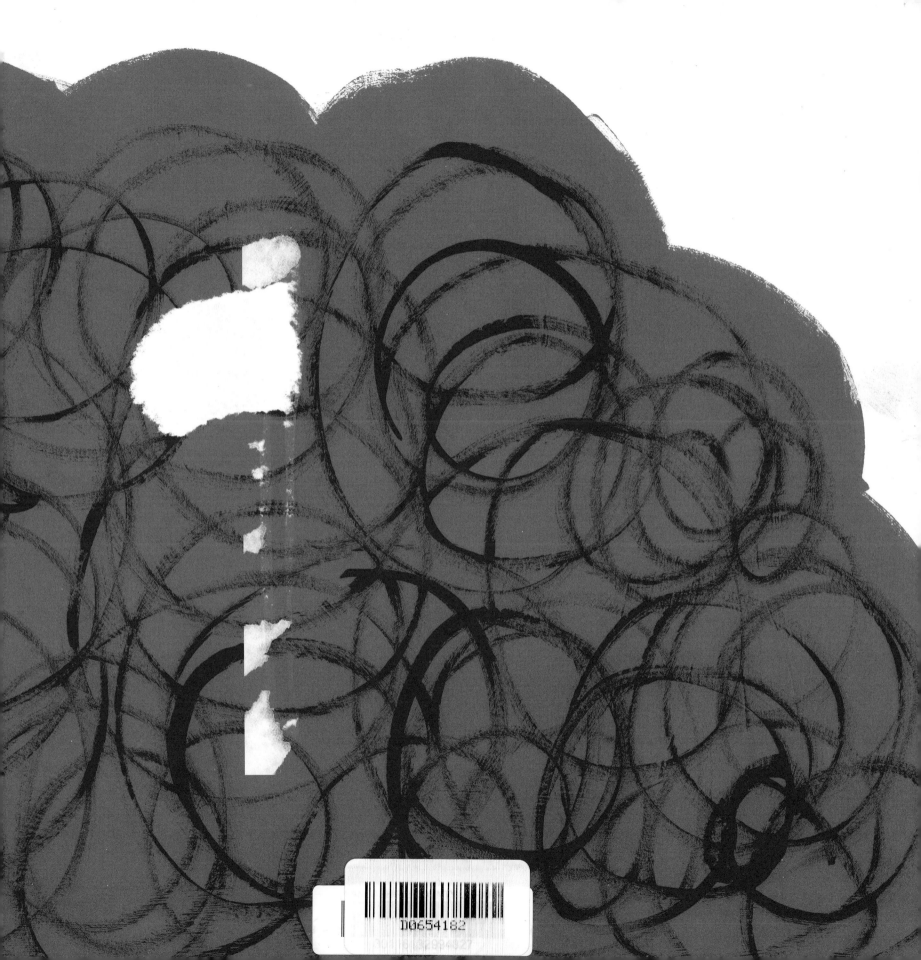

For Mr. Schu, who's never horrible.
— A.D.

For Lydia, O Bear, and Chomper.
— Z.O.

SNAP!

HORRIBLE BEAR!

Written by **Ame Dyckman**   Illustrated by **Zachariah OHora**

ANDERSEN PRESS

A girl peeked into Bear's cave.

She reached —
but he rolled.

CRUNCH!

HORRIBLE BEAR!

the girl shouted.

The girl stomped down the mountain.

She stomped through the meadow.

HORRIBLE BEAR!

She stomped all the way home.

Bear was indignant.

"I'M not horrible!" he said.

"SHE barged in!"

"SHE made a ruckus!"

"SHE woke ME up!"   "How would SHE like it if — "

Bear got an idea.

It was a Horrible Bear idea.

Bear practised barging.

He practised making a ruckus.

He practised waking someone up.

HORRIBLE BEAR!

Bat squeaked.

"Perfect!" Bear said.

Bear stomped out of his cave.

The girl stomped into her room.

But she was too upset to nap.
So, the girl tried drawing.

She tried reading.

She tried talking to the best listener she knew.

THAT HORRIBLE BEAR!

"He broke my —"

RIP!

Suddenly, her stuffie couldn't listen as well as before.

"I didn't mean to!" the girl cried.

"Oh."

Meanwhile... Bear stomped down the mountain.

He stomped through the meadow.

He stomped straight to the girl's front door —

which opened.

I'M SORRY!

the girl said.

And all the horrible
went right out of Bear.

Bear patted.

He wiped.

He got another idea.

It was a Sweet Bear idea.

"Thank you, Bear,"
the girl whispered.

She had a
Sweet Bear idea,
too.

Bear and the girl skipped through the meadow.

They bounced up the mountain.

And together, they patched everything up.

Even the kite.

Nothing was horrible at all...

for the moment.

AUTHOR'S NOTE

I lost a kite once. The string snapped, and my new kite sailed away — maybe into a bear's cave. I hope the bear liked it.
— *Ame Dyckman*

ARTIST'S NOTE

The art for *Horrible Bear!* was created using acrylic paint on 90-pound acid-free Stonehenge printing paper. The story inspired me to buy lots of kites and overcome my fear of using the colour purple.
— *Zachariah OHora*

First published in Great Britain in 2016 by Andersen Press Ltd.,
20 Vauxhall Bridge Road, London SW1V 2SA.
Originally published by Little, Brown and Company, Hachette Book Group,
1290 Avenue of the Americas, New York, NY 10104, USA
Text copyright © 2016 by Ame Dyckman
Illustrations copyright © 2016 by Zachariah OHora
The rights of Ame Dyckman and Zachariah OHora to be identified as
the author and illustrator of this work have been asserted by them
in accordance with the Copyright, Designs and Patents Act, 1988.
All rights reserved.
Printed and bound in China.

1 3 5 7 9 10 8 6 4 2
British Library Cataloguing in Information Data available.
ISBN 978 178344 481 6 (hardback)
ISBN 978 1 78344 514 1 (paperback)